T0193281

The Queen's Lost Unicorn

LUKE MANGAN

To order additional copies of this book, contact:
Xlibris
844-714-8691
www.Xlibris.com
Orders@Xlibris.com

ISBN: Softcover   978-1-6698-2639-2
        EBook   978-1-6698-2638-5

Print information available on the last page

Rev. date: 09/27/2023

The Queen's Lost Unicorn.

Once upon a time, in a magical land. There lived the Queen of the fairies in her grand castle on a hilltop. The Queen wore a gold crown and a purple gown. The unicorns lived happily and peacefully with the fairies. Across the river from her kingdom was a spooky dark forest that no one ever went into.

One-day two unicorns went to get a drink from the river. Lavender, a curious unicorn, said to Sparkles the unicorn, do you ever wonder what is in the deep dark forest that no one has ever explored.

Sparkles said I heard no one ever goes into the dark forest. However, I am brave and clever said, Lavender. Therefore, I should go and explore. Lavender, the curious unicorn, walked across the shallow river. He went into the forest to see what was in it. He looked at different colored flowers and ate some wild berries, and the blackberries were sweet.

Lavender continued to walk down the path and came upon an old gray stone castle by a waterfall. As he went deeper into the forest, he got lost.

Suddenly he heard a noise from behind him. He turned around and saw a stranger. Do not be afraid I am just a lonely little friendly gnome.

The gnome said, wow, you are a strange-looking creature, a horse with a horn on it. I am a unicorn.

The gnome said I will show you around. The unicorn said, are you the one who says hoo at night? No, those are the birds called owls.

The gnome and the unicorn have fun and play games together all day long.

When it got dark, the unicorn said, I have to go home now.

The gnome said that it is too dark to travel now. But my horn glows makes a good night light. The gnome said it is still too dangerous to travel at night. The following day, they get up and eat breakfast. He says I have to go home now. The gnome said you should not go so soon. You are my new friend you need to stay with me. We can play few more games, and so they did.

So I need to leave now, it is getting late.

The gnome said let's just do one more quick game. The unicorn said, ok.

This is called the lasso game. The gnome lasso the unicorn with a rope. The gnome tied up the unicorn in the cave underneath his castle. Now you will stay with me and be my friend.

The unicorn was sad and said this is not a way to treat a friend.

I do not want you to leave me here alone again.

Meanwhile, the Queen sent out two noble knights to go into the forest to look for Lavender. The knights followed the path like a road deep into the middle of the forest. They find the unicorn in the gnome's castle.

The Queen of the fairies has requested the return of her unicorn by royal order. One of the knights said to the gnome.

The gnome sadly said I do not want you to take my new friend away.

The knight said you could see that Lavender the unicorn is sad. Because his horn stopped glowing. Where are you from? I have been lost in these woods for a very long time, and I do not remember. The gnome said that I am lonely without a friend here. One of the knights said, you should come back with us to the Queen's kingdom. The gnome said, yes, I will go with you to Queen's realm. Then I will not be alone anymore.

They all made the journey back to the Queen's kingdom. There was bright light sun and rainbows in the sky. The gnome was happy in his new home, with all his new friends. They all lived happily ever after. The end.

Printed in the United States
by Baker & Taylor Publisher Services